Words to Know Before

adventurous
built
donate
famished
favorite
flashlight
flowers
ranger
recognize
shelter
suggested
thrown

www.rourkeeducationalmedia.com

Edited by Precious McKenzie
Illustrated by Robin Koontz
Art Direction and Page Layout by Renee Brady

Library of Congress PCN Data

Robin Hood / Robin Koontz
ISBN 978-1-61810-192-1 (hard cover) (alk. paper)
ISBN 978-1-61810-325-3 (soft cover)
Library of Congress Control Number: 2012936792

Rourke Educational Media
Printed in China, Artwood Press Limited,
  Shenzhen, China

rourkeeducationalmedia.com

customerservice@rourkeeducationalmedia.com • PO Box 643328 Vero Beach, Florida 32964

Robin Hood

Written and Illustrated
by Robin Koontz

The Band of Merry Hikers was hiking on their favorite trail in Sherwood Forest.
"We've been on this trail many times before," said Theo the raccoon.

"Let's try a new trail," Theo suggested.
"This trail looks adventurous," said Maxie.

"We will need to find our way back," Lawrence said. "I know just what to do. We can mark the trail so we don't get lost," Maxie said.

"Mark it with what?" Lawrence asked.

"We can use our forks and spoons," Theo suggested.

7

The Band of Merry Hikers tied forks and spoons to the trees all along the trail. The trail ended at a lake.

"I will gather flowers," said Theo.

"I will paint a picture," said Maxie.

"I will watch for bears," said Lawrence.

"You are a bear," said Theo.

"Not all bears are nice," Lawrence said.

9

The Band of Merry Hikers headed back.
The trail zigged left. It zagged right.

"Where did our forks and spoons go?" cried Theo.
"They are gone," cried Maxie.
"We are lost!" cried Lawrence.

The Band of Merry Hikers walked and walked.
"I'm famished!" cried Maxie.
They stopped to eat. Theo had a big pot of pudding.
"We have no spoons!" said Theo.

12

"Help!" Maxie called.
"Help! Help!" cried Theo.
It started to rain.
"HELLLLLP!" they all cried.

"Hello!" a voice called. A ranger shined his flashlight on the Band of Merry Hikers. "Come with me," he said.

15

"This is a very nice shelter!" said Lawrence.
"I built it myself," said the ranger.

"Have some soup," said the ranger.
"Hey, I recognize that spoon!" said Theo.

"I found lots of spoons and forks today," said the ranger.
"I thought that someone littered."

"We tied them to trees to find our way home," said Maxie. "I'm sorry," said the ranger. "I collect things that are thrown away and donate them to others who need them."

"That makes you like Robin Hood!" said Theo.
"Robin Hood gave things to anyone who needed them."
"I like the name Robin Hood!" said the ranger.

He led the Band of Merry Hikers back to the main trail.
"Please stay on the marked trails," said Ranger
Robin Hood.
"We will!" said the Band of Merry Hikers.

After Reading Activities

You and the Story...

How did the Band of Merry Hikers get their name?

Can you remember a story where somebody marked a trail to find their way home?

What should you do if you get lost in the woods?

Some ideas: Hug a tree. Call for help. Stay warm and dry.

Words You Know Now...

Write each word on a piece of paper. Circle the four nouns. Use two of the nouns in a sentence. Can you write another sentence using the other two nouns?

adventurous	favorite	recognize
built	flashlight	shelter
donate	flowers	suggested
famished	ranger	thrown

You Could...Mark a Trail

- Decide where you want to walk and tell an adult.

- Use pieces of string, ribbon, or colorful tape to mark your way.

- Tie or stick your markers to trees and bushes.

- Walk back the same way, following your markers.

- Be sure to remove the markers and save them to use again on a new trail.

About the Author and Illustrator

Robin Koontz loves to write and illustrate stories that make kids laugh. Robin lives with her husband and various critters in the Coast Range mountains of western Oregon. She shares her office space with Jeep the dog, who gives her most of her ideas.

Ask The Author!
www.rem4students.com